Agape's Gift

Book Three of JuJu's Fairies
Concept by Julie (JuJu) Eckstein

Written by

The Notorious Mrs. D

Bible verses are taken from the English Standard Version (ESV)
The Holy Bible, English Standard Version. ESV® Text Edition: 2016. Copyright
© 2001 by Crossway Bibles, a publishing ministry of Good News Publishers.

Bible verses are listed in order of appearance in an appendix at the end of the book.

DEDICATION

All of my writing is dedicated to my Lord Jesus, the Son of the Living God.
You gave us your life, so we could be in yours.
Thank you for being the love of my life!

In addition, this book series is dedicated to my sister in Christ, Julie Eckstein, creator of the original concept *A Day in the Life of a Fairy* and the character Fairy Clementine. Thank you for the opportunity to bless you by expanding this concept into a budding book series. I pray that many are blessed through the wisdom imparted by these books. I love you JuJu!

.

ABOUT THE AUTHOR

Rebekah Duchesneau earned her title *The Notorious Mrs. D* while working in special education. The term *notorious* because she pushed students to achieve more than they believed they could; *Mrs. D* because the adults had trouble pronouncing her name. Rebekah felt if she could do anything for her students, it was to teach them to rise above their hindrances and discover their strengths; but more importantly, she tried to instill in them a greater sense of self-worth. Rebekah is known by her coworkers and students for her quirky sense of humor. She confesses being a real smart aleck. Her hope is that those reading her books will come away with some encouragement, some giggles, and a smile.

ABOUT JUJU'S FAIRIES

Fairy Clementine was a concept developed by Rebekah's good friend and sister in Christ, Julie Eckstein. After reading through her drafts, Rebekah encouraged her that this would someday make a fun book. Julie agreed, and they embarked on making this dream come true. Some years later, Rebekah was inspired to expand Fairy Clementine's story. She gave her a family by the name of Plenty which includes 8 sisters. They all clean homes (in secret) for those in need. The focus of the series is *The Fruit of the Spirit* as depicted in Galatians 5 of the Bible. Chapters and verses are indexed in an appendix. The message of these books is beneficial for both believers and non-believers. Rebekah has a firm belief that God's Word does not return void (Isaiah 55:11) and therefore brings life, revelation and encouragement to the reader. Good seed is planted in the reading of these books.

ABOUT THE ILLUSTRATIONS AND CHARACTERS

As for the illustration of the characters; Rebekah says she followed no strategy. After a couple years, lack of funds motivated her to create them herself. She does not consider herself an artist. She says the illustrations are rough, but fun. There was no consideration for race or ethnicity. The skin color of all the characters is *paper*. Just *paper*. She leaves it up to the reader to decide what color the characters should be.

Galatians 5:22

But the fruit of the Spirit is love, joy, peace, patience, kindness, goodness, faithfulness, gentleness, self-control; against such things there is no law.

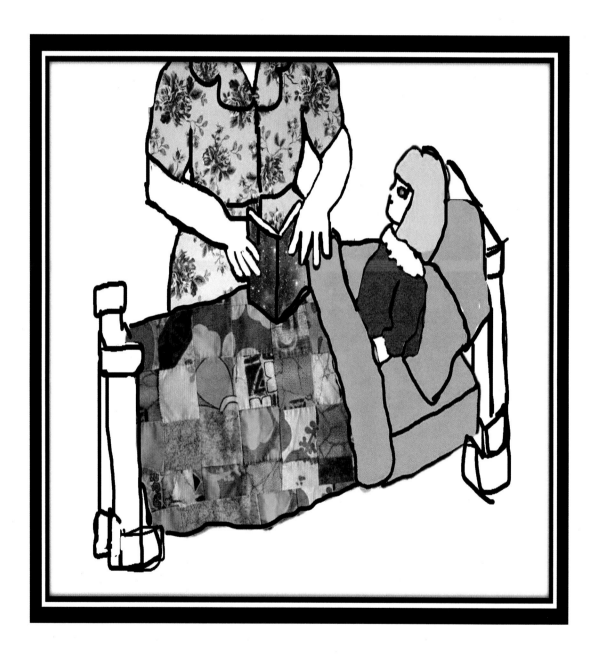

AGAPE'S GIFT

The Love of Philoppy

"...and that's what became of the Gumnus of Flamalachi Springs. Alright Juju, get some rest." Grammy Ann gently kissed Juju on the forehead and turned out the lamp. "Sweet dreams Juju. I love you."

"I love you, too, Grammy Ann." Thinking about the story, Juju snuggled down into her covers. Her sleepy eyes began to close.

Suddenly, Juju was startled at the sight of a beautiful grassy area with lots of trees. She saw a sign that she remembered seeing before. It said, "Very Merry Fairy Land." Off in the distance, Juju saw what appeared to be a whole village of very happy (merry) fairies.

These fairies were so happy because of their special way of helping people in secret. Some fairy families were good at fixing things. Others made toys. Still others were gardeners. No matter how hard they worked, they were all very merry.

Juju then saw a tiny beautiful cottage with a plaque bearing the name, "The Plenty Family." Mama and Papa Plenty were inside rejoicing over the arrival of their new fairy baby daughters.

"Oh Papa, this one has beautiful red hair. What shall we name her?" Mama queried.

Papa replied, "I can see the love of the Creator beaming from her little face."

"Let's call her Agape'!" declared Mama.

"Perfect! Agape' is a special kind of love that God gives *and* is the first of the Fruit of the Spirit!" cried Papa.

Mama agreed, "What a great way to thank God for blessing us with this fairy-sweet child!"

"Fruit?" Juju wondered. "What does he mean by fruit?" Then Juju remembered something Grammy Ann taught her about The Fruit of the Spirit (not the fruit we eat). She said, "The Fruit of God's Spirit is what comes from talking to God and learning from Him. As you get to know Him more, you grow in the fruit of *love, joy, peace, patience, kindness, goodness, faithfulness, gentleness, and self-control*. These are all good things that help us to love others like God loves all of us."[1]

Suddenly, Juju saw a beautiful young fairy emerging from the Plenty house.

Papa Plenty remarked, "Our little Agape' is so grown up! Literally, just this morning we were changing her diapers. Now look at her!" (Fairy babies grow really, really fast!)

Agape' was preparing for her first assignment in helping someone. She was obviously nervous. Juju learned that the Plenty family loved cleaning houses in secret for those unable to do it for themselves.

But Agape' had nothing to worry about. She learned exactly what to do AND how to stay out of sight in Fairy School. No fairy ever wants to be caught doing their good deeds! They do things to help others, not to get praise. The Creator wants us to do good and help others, expecting nothing in return.[2]

Agape' arrived at Mrs. Ruddyduppy's home.

Once the house was empty, Agape' set about her task. With all the love she had in her heart, she gave the house the best top-to-bottom cleaning ever. Then, just as Mrs. Ruddyduppy came home, Agape' slipped out the door!

As she was leaving, she heard loud sounds from down the street. She saw a large globby-looking creature wandering up to the store fronts. It seemed to be looking for food. The shop owners didn't want this thing around, so they yelled and threw things trying to scare it away. What an awful scene!

The beast hurried down the sidewalk and ran into Agape'. Her wings became entangled in its gooey covering. The frightened creature dashed in and out of alleyways while Agape' struggled to get free. Finally, it crashed into a pile of trashcans.

What was Agape' to do? How would she get unstuck from this gooey thing? She wondered if this could be the Gumnus of Flamalachi Springs she had heard about? After all, the creature *was strange*, AND they *were* in Flamalachi Springs.

Finally, Agape' broke free from her gooey bondage and landed on the ground next to the beast. It towered over her tiny fairy body. Black-brown goo covered its matted hair. A boot and a child's pinwheel were stuck to its head. Trailing from its tail was a paper cup and a deflated balloon bouquet. The colorful plastic weights from the balloons made clattering sounds that startled the poor beast whenever it moved.

The creature growled at Agape'. This thing was as big to her as an elephant is to a child. If it were to attack, she wouldn't stand a chance. Agape' stood still, not sure what to do. Then, to her amazement, the creature suddenly ran away.

Agape' didn't know what to think. What was this disgusting thing? And why were people so mean to it?

Agape' decided to learn about the poor creature. This would not be an easy task. Afterall, since fairies were not to be seen, she couldn't talk with the people there.

She decided to do some research on the Fairy-net. Agape' found articles from the VMF Times (Very Merry Fairyland Times) that reported sightings of the beast. Apparently, the creature just appeared out of nowhere, scaring people and leaving nasty goo wherever it went. Gradually it became called *The Gumnus of Flamalachi Springs*.

This was all very interesting, but there had to be more to the story.

Agape' decided to ask the fairy elder in her village for help. His name was *Gary the Fairy Elder*. "Mr. Gary the Fairy Elder sir, please tell me about the Gumnus of Flamalachi Springs."

"My child, the Gumnus is not the monster that people think. Approach him with the love of God for which you are named. Your name describes the deep love The Creator has for all his people. This is the kind of love where a person would give his life to save the life of another. This is exactly what He did to save His people from their sin. There is no greater love.[3]

"Agape' love is one of the Fruit of the Spirit that comes from spending time with God and working to live a life in Him.

Approach this creature with this kind of love and care and you will learn everything you want to know and more."

Indeed, the key to understanding this beast was in her name. Agape' wasn't just to be nice to the creature but be willing to put her needs aside to help it.

Trusting what Gary the Fairy Elder had said, Agape' decided to try to make friends with the Gumnus. But how? When she saw it the first time, it seemed to be looking for food. Maybe she could offer it some food. This could be dangerous considering her tiny size.

The next day, Agape' carried a small biscuit in her bag. She looked all around as she flew home, hoping to meet it again. Suddenly a tree branch fell onto a power line causing the live pieces to drape across the road. Agape' was headed right for it! If she were to touch that live wire, the electricity in it could shock her!

Suddenly, the Gumnus came out of nowhere and lunged at Agape'! She was sure it wanted to eat her! But in lunging at her, it dove right into Agape', knocking her away from the live power line!

Agape' was saved! She had been on her way to help the poor creature and yet it put its own safety aside to save her. She felt so badly for the poor thing and wanted so much to help.

From where she had landed, Agape' couldn't see the Gumnus. There didn't appear to be any movement amongst the rubble. Was this the end of the Gumnus of Flamalachi Springs? Did this sad thing give up its own life for someone it did not even know?

As the smoke cleared Agape' saw, scattered all over the road, chunks of the

black-brown goo and trash that had

previously covered the Gumnus.

Then, she saw movement in the pile. Out from the clutter emerged a white and black little dog! And it was just her size, too!

What happened to the Gumnus? The shock from the power line exploded all the junk off of him. But then, something even more amazing happened; he shrank! And now he was a beautiful fairy-sized little dog!

Agape' sounded, "Oh, my goodness! Oh, you poor thing! Come here! Let me hug you! You risked your life to save mine!"

The little dog was hungry and weak, and unsure of what Agape' might do. Afterall, so many people had been unkind to him. But Agape' was different and HE was different!

He staggered toward Agape'. She scooped him up into her arms and held him tight. As she did, hundreds of bubbly red hearts floated up from them into the air. All at once his black spots became little red hearts!

"Oh, how adorable! Will you be my doggy?" Agape' spouted.

Agape' was rewarded with wet sloppy kisses of gratitude!

The pup jumped out of her arms and ran little circles around her, jumping and barking with joy!

"You're such a cute little thing! I'm going to call you Philoppy because of your adorable floppy ears!"

And just like that; all the sadness was gone. The stray little dog now had a home. No more fear of strangers. No more worry about being fed. He was safe and secure with Agape. AND Agape' was safe and secure because of Philoppy's act of self-sacrifice. He nearly lost his life to save hers. And that's what became of the Gumnus of Flamalachi Springs.

Suddenly JuJu sat up in bed! Confused, she wondered, "Oh wow! What a dream!"

Grammy Ann walked by the door and saw Juju sitting up. "Juju are you awake?" she asked.

Juju responded, "Yes Grammy Ann. I dreamed about the Gumnus of Flamalachi Springs. It was a little scary."

"How so, Juju?"

"The Gumnus saved Agape' from touching a power line."

"A power line!? Who's Agape'?"

"She's a housecleaning fairy. Did you know housecleaning fairies grow up, like, in minutes?"

"In minutes? What?"

"Yeah, it's really cool! Anyway, agape' means special love like when a person gives up their life for someone."

"That's true Juju. Agape', or love, is the first of the Fruit of the Spirit. There are 9; *love, joy, peace, patience, kindness, goodness, faithfulness, gentleness, and self-control.*[1] These help us live a happier life, even when times are bad."

"Can I have agape' love too? What if I'm too scared?" asked Juju.

Grammy replied, "The Fruit of the Spirit are available to all God's children. They grow in us as we spend more time with God and try to live for Him.[1] Now Juju, you don't have to do like the Gumnus and give up your life. Agape' also means placing other's needs ahead of your own."

Grammy Ann gave Juju a comforting hug and a kiss, and said, "I love that you know about agape' love and the other Fruit of the Spirit. This is something that everyone can have when they spend time with God in prayer."

"Yes Grammy Ann, and I'm glad that the Gumnus turned into a cute little doggy for Agape' to love. He deserved her love after all he'd been through and saving her life."

"Juju, did you know God IS love?[5] He wants us to love each other like He loves us. Did you know that God gave of Himself when He sent His Son Jesus to give His life to save us from punishment for our sin? That is how much God and Jesus love all of us.[4] That is how agape' love works. The Bible says, "Greater love has no one than this, that someone lay down his life for his friends.""[3]

"I learned about that in church. I try to remember to tell everyone I know so someday they can go to Heaven. Grammy Ann, what's Heaven like?"

"Juju, it's where God and Jesus and all the angels live. It's a beautiful place where there's no sadness, sickness or pain. Jesus loves His people and God wishes that no one would miss out on going to Heaven. Every time you tell someone, you give them a chance to get there, too. Try to sleep now, Honey." encouraged Grammy Ann.

"I love you, Grammy Ann."

"I love you, too, Juju. Goodnight."

Grammy Ann kissed Juju on the forehead and tucked her into bed.

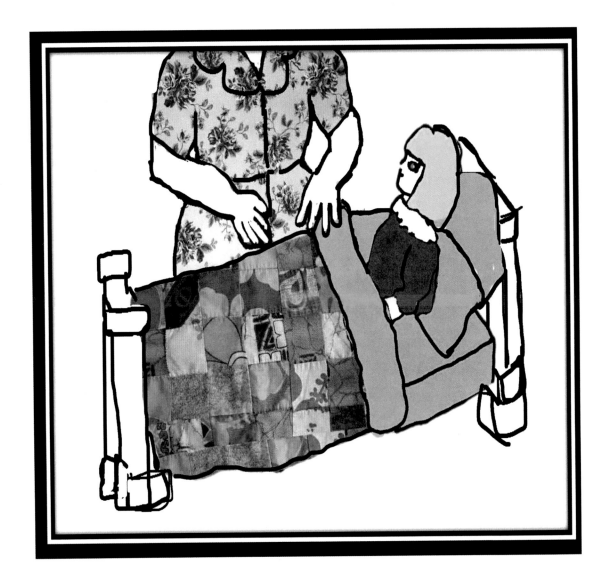

How about you? Do you know that Jesus loved all people everywhere so much that he gave up his life so they could live with him forever? If you would like to someday go to Heaven and live with him forever, then pray this prayer:

Jesus, I believe you are the Son of God. I believe you died and rose again for the bad things everyone has ever done. I know I have done bad things. Please forgive me and let me someday live with you in Heaven.[5] Thank you for saving me. Amen.

Okay, now what? Well, the next thing to do is find a book called the Bible and ask someone to help you learn about it. The more you read from it, the more you will learn about Jesus' love for you and the wonderful person God made you to be.

Appendix

The following are Bible verses referenced or eluded to in the story. All verses were taken from the English Standard Version (ESV) unless otherwise indicated.

1. Galatians 5:22-23 [22] But the fruit of the Spirit is love, joy, peace, patience, kindness, goodness, faithfulness, [23] gentleness, self-control; against such things there is no law.

2. Matthew 6:1-4 "Beware of practicing your righteousness before other people in order to be seen by them, for then you will have no reward from your Father who is in heaven. [2] "Thus, when you give to the needy, sound no trumpet before you, as the hypocrites do in the synagogues and in the streets, that they may be praised by others. Truly, I say to you, they have received their reward. [3] But when you give to the needy, do not let your left hand know what your right hand is doing, [4] so that your giving may be in secret. And your Father who sees in secret will reward you.

3. John 15:13 [3] Greater love has no one than this, that someone lay down his life for his friends.

4. John 3:16 "For God so loved the world, that he gave his only Son, that whoever believes in him should not perish but have eternal life.

5. 1 John 4:7-8 "Beloved, let us love one another, for love is from God, and whoever loves has been born of God and knows God. [8] Anyone who does not love does not know God, because God is love."

Meet JuJu's Fairies

Agape (Love)	Aleeza (Joy)	Paz (Peace)
Grizelda (Patience)	Charity (Kindness)	Lila (Goodness)
Fidessa (Faithfulness)	Clementine (Gentleness)	Sophie (Self Control)

Each sister has her own book dedicated to the characteristic they represent.